Usborne Farmyard Tales

The New Pony

Heather Amery

Illustrated by Stephen Cartwright

Language consultant: Betty Root
Series editor: Jenny Tyler

There is a little yellow duck to find on every page.

This is Apple Tree Farm.

This is Mrs. Boot, the farmer. She has two children, called Poppy and Sam, and a dog called Rusty.

Mr. Boot, Poppy and Sam go for a walk.

They see a new pony. "She belongs to Mr. Stone, who's just bought Old Gate Farm," says Mr. Boot.

The pony looks sad.

Her coat is rough and dirty. She looks hungry.
It looks as though no one takes care of her.

Poppy tries to stroke the pony.

"She's not very friendly," says Sam. "Mr. Stone says she's bad tempered," says Mr. Boot.

Poppy feeds the pony.

Every day, Poppy takes her apples and carrots.
But she always stays on the other side of the gate.

One day, Poppy takes Sam with her.

They cannot see the pony anywhere. The field
looks empty. "Where is she?" says Sam.

Poppy and Sam open the gate.

Rusty runs into the field. Poppy and Sam are a bit scared. "We must find the pony," says Poppy.

"There she is," says Sam.

The pony has caught her head collar in the fence.
She has been eating the grass on the other side.

Poppy and Sam run home to Mr. Boot.

"Please come and help us, Dad," says Poppy. "The pony is caught in the fence. She will hurt herself."

Mr. Boot walks up to the pony.

He unhooks the pony's head collar from the fence.
"She's not hurt," says Mr. Boot.

"The pony's chasing us."

"Quick, run," says Sam. "It's all right," says Poppy, patting the pony. "She just wants to be friends."

They see an angry man. It is Mr. Stone.

"Leave my pony alone," says Mr. Stone. "And get out of my field." He waves his stick at Poppy.

The pony is afraid of Mr. Stone.

Mr. Stone tries to hit the pony with his stick. "I'm going to get rid of that nasty animal," he says.

Poppy grabs his arm.

"You mustn't hit the pony," she cries. "Come on Poppy," says Mr. Boot. "Let's go home."

Next day, there's a surprise for Poppy.

The pony is at Apple Tree Farm. "We've bought her for you," says Mrs. Boot. "Thank you," says Poppy.

Cover design by Hannah Ahmed   Digital manipulation by Nelupa Hussain

This edition first published in 2004 by Usborne Publishing Ltd, 83-85 Saffron Hill, London EC1N 8RT, England. www.usborne.com